Frederick George Scott

**My Lattice**

And Other Poems

Frederick George Scott

**My Lattice**
*And Other Poems*

ISBN/EAN: 9783744773034

Printed in Europe, USA, Canada, Australia, Japan

Cover: Foto ©Andreas Hilbeck / pixelio.de

More available books at **www.hansebooks.com**

# MY LATTICE

## AND OTHER POEMS

# MY LATTICE

## *AND OTHER POEMS*

BY

## FREDERICK GEORGE SCOTT

AUTHOR OF "THE SOUL'S QUEST, AND OTHER POEMS," "ELTON
HAZLEWOOD," ETC.

TORONTO:
WILLIAM BRIGGS.
C. W. COATES, Montreal.        S. F. HUESTIS, Halifax.
1894.

# CONTENTS.

## SONNETS.

# MY LATTICE.

## MY LATTICE.

My lattice looks upon the North,
   The winds are cool that enter :
At night I see the stars come forth,
   Arcturus in the centre.

The curtain down my casement drawn
   Is dewy mist, which lingers
Until my maid, the rosy dawn,
   Uplifts it with her fingers.

The sparrows are my matin-bell,
   Each day my heart rejoices,
When, from the trellis where they dwell,
   They call me with their voices.

# MY LATTICE.

Then, as I dream with half-shut eye,
  Without a sound or motion,
To me that little square of sky
  Becomes a boundless ocean.

And straight my soul unfurls its sails
  That blue sky-sea to sever,
My fancies are the noiseless gales
  That waft it on forever.

I sail into the depths of space
  And leave the clouds behind me,
I pass the old moon's hiding-place,
  The sun's rays cannot find me.

I sail beyond the solar light,
  Beyond the constellations,
Across the voids where loom in sight
  New systems and creations.

I pass great worlds of silent stone,
  Whence light and life have vanished,
Which wander on to tracts unknown,
  In lonely exile banished.

I meet with spheres of fiery mist
  Which warm me as I enter,
Where— ruby, gold and amethyst
  The rainbow lights concentre.

And on I sail into the vast,
  New wonders aye discerning,
Until my mind is lost at last,
  And, suddenly returning,

I feel the wind which, cool as dew,
  Upon my face is falling,
And see again my patch of blue
  And hear the sparrows calling.

# SAMSON.

Plunged in night, I sit alone
Eyeless on this dungeon stone,
Naked, shaggy and unkempt,
Dreaming dreams no soul hath dreamt.

Rats and vermin round my feet
Play unharmed, companions sweet :
Spiders weave me overhead
Silken curtains for my bed.

Day by day the mould I smell
Of this fungus-blistered cell ;
Nightly in my haunted sleep
O'er my face the lizards creep.

Gyves of iron scrape and burn
Wrists and ankles when I turn,
And my collared neck is raw
With the teeth of brass that gnaw.

God of Israel, canst Thou see
All my fierce captivity?
Do Thy sinews feel my pains?
Hearest Thou the clanking chains?

Thou who madest me so fair,
Strong and buoyant as the air,
Tall and noble as a tree,
With the passions of the sea,

Swift as horse upon my feet,
Fierce as lion in my heat,
Rending, like a wisp of hay,
All that dared withstand my way,

Canst Thou see me through the gloom
Of this subterranean tomb,—
Blinded tiger in his den,
Once the lord and prince of men?

Clay was I; the potter Thou
With Thy thumb-nail smooth'dst my brow,
Roll'dst the spittle-moistened sands
Into limbs between Thy hands.

Thou didst pour into my blood
Fury of the fire and flood,
And upon the boundless skies
Thou didst first unclose my eyes.

And my breath of life was flame,
God-like from the source it came,
Whirling round like furious wind,
Thoughts upgathered in the mind.

Strong Thou mad'st me, till at length
All my weakness was my strength ;
Tortured am I, blind and wrecked,
For a faulty architect.

From the woman at my side,
Was I woman-like to hide
What she asked me, as if fear
Could my iron heart come near?

Nay, I scorned and scorn again
Cowards who their tongues restrain ;
Cared I no more for Thy laws
Than a wind of scattered straws.

When the earth quaked at my name
And my blood was all aflame,
Who was I to lie, and cheat
Her who clung about my feet?

From Thy open nostrils blow
Wind and tempest, rain and snow;
Dost Thou curse them on their course,
For the fury of their force?

Tortured am I, wracked and bowed,
But the soul within is proud ;
Dungeon fetters cannot still
Forces of the tameless will.

Israel's God, come down and see
All my fierce captivity ;
Let Thy sinews feel my pains,
With Thy fingers lift my chains.

Then, with thunder loud and wild,
Comfort Thou Thy rebel child,
And with lightning split in twain
Loveless heart and sightless brain.

Give me splendour in my death—
Not this sickening dungeon breath,
Creeping down my blood like slime,
Till it wastes me in my prime.

Give me back for one blind hour,
Half my former rage and power,
And some giant crisis send,
Meet to prove a hero's end.

Then, O God, Thy mercy show—
Crush him in the overthrow
At whose life they scorn and point,
By its greatness out of joint.

# IN VIA MORTIS.

O YE great company of dead that sleep
   Under the world's green rind, I come to you,
With warm, soft limbs, with eyes that laugh and weep,
    Heart strong to love, and brain pierced through
        and through
      With thoughts whose rapid lightnings make my
        day —
     To you my life-stream courses on its way
Through margin-shallows of the eternal deep.

And naked shall I come among you, shorn
   Of all life's vanities, its light and power,
Its earthly lusts, its petty hate and scorn,
    The gifts and gold I treasured for an hour ;
      And even from this house of flesh laid bare,
      A soul transparent as heat-quivering air,
Into your fellowship I shall be born.

I know you not, great forms of giant kings,
   Who held dominion in your iron hands,

Who toyed with battles and all valorous things,
  Counting yourselves as gods when on the sands
    Ye piled the earth's rock fragments in an heap
    To mark and guard the grandeur of your sleep,
And quaffed the cup which death, our mother, brings.

I know you not, great warriors, who have fought
  When blood flowed like a river at your feet,
And each death which your thunderous sword-strokes
      wrought,
  Than love's wild rain of kisses was more sweet.
    I know you not, great minds, who with the pen
    Have graven on the fiery hearts of men
Hopes that breed hope and thoughts that kindle
      thought.

But ye are there, ingathered in the realm
  Where tongueless spirits speak from heart to heart,
And eyeless mariners without a helm
  Steer down the seas where ever close and part
    The windless clouds ; and all ye know is this,
    Ye are not as ye were in pain or bliss,
But a strange numbness doth all thought o'erwhelm.

And I shall meet you, O ye mighty dead,
   Come late into your kingdom through the gates
Of one fierce anguish whitherto I tread,
   With heart that now forgets, now meditates
      Upon the wide fields stretching far away
      Where the dead wander past the bounds of day,
Past life, past death, past every pain and dread.

Oft, when the winter sun slopes down to rest
   Across the long, crisp fields of gilded white,
And without sound upon earth's level breast
   The grey tide floods around of drowning night,
      A whisper, like a distant battle's roll
      Heard over mountains, creeps into my soul,
And there I entertain it like a guest.

It is the echo of your former pains,
   Great dead, who lie so still beneath the ground :
Its voice is as the night wind after rains,
   The flight of eagle wings which once were bound,
      And as I listen in the starlit air
      My spirit waxeth stronger than despair,
Till in your might I break life's prison chains.

B

Then mount I swiftly to your dark abodes,
  Invisible, beyond sight's reach, where now ye dwell
In houses wrought of dreams on dusky roads
  Which lead in mazes whither none may tell,
    For they who thread them faint beside the way,
    And ever as they pass through twilight grey
Doubt walks beside them and a terror goads.

And there the great dead welcome me and bring
  Their cups of tasteless pleasure to my mouth :
Here am I little worth, there am I king,
  For pulsing life still slakes my spirit's drouth,
    And he who yet doth hold the gift of life
    Is mightier than the heroes of past strife
Who have been mowed in death's great harvesting.

And here and there along the silent streets
  I see some face I knew, perchance I loved :
And as I call it each blank wall repeats
  The uttered name, and swift the form hath moved
    And heedless of me passes on and on,
    Till lo, the vision from my sight hath gone
Softly as night at touch of dawn retreats.

Yet must life's vision fade and I shall come,
  O mighty dead, into your hidden land,
When these eyes see not and these lips are dumb,
  And all life's flowers slip from this nerveless hand ;
    Then will ye gather round me like a tide
    And with your faces the strange scenery hide,
While your weird music doth each sense benumb.

So would I live this life's brief span, great dead,
  As ye once lived it, with an iron will,
A heart of steel to conquer, a mind fed
  On richest hopes and purposes, until
    Well pleased ye set for me a royal throne,
    And welcome as confederate with your own
The soul gone from me on my dying bed.

# THOR.

HERE stood the great god Thor,
   There he planted his foot,
And the whole world shook, from the shore
   To the circle of mountains God put
For its crown in the days of yore.

The waves of the sea uprose,
   The trees of the wood were uptorn,
Down from the Alps' crown of snows
   The glacial avalanche borne
Thundered at daylight's close.

But the moon-lady curled at his feet,
   Like a smoke which will not stir,
When the summer hills swoon with the heat,
   Till his passion was centred on her,
And the shame of his yielding grew sweet.

Empty the moon-lady's car,
 And idly it floated away,
Tipped up as she left it afar,
 Pale in the red death of day,
With its nether lip turned to a star.


Fearful the face of the god,
 Stubborn with sense of his power,
The seas would roll back at his nod
 And the thunder-voiced thunder-clouds lower,
While the lightning he broke as a rod.


Fearful his face was in war,
 Iron with fixed look of hate,
Through the battle-smoke thick and the roar
 He strode with invincible weight
Till the legions fell back before Thor.


But the white thing that curled at his feet
 Rose up slowly beside him like mist,
Indefinite, wan, incomplete,
 Till she touched the rope veins on his wrist
And love pulsed to his heart with a beat.

Then he looked, and from under her hair,
  As from out of a mist grew her eyes,
And firmer her flesh was and fair
  With the tint of the sorrowful skies,
Sun-widowed and veiled with thin air.


She seemed of each lovable thing
  The soul that infused it with grace,
Her thoughts were the song the birds sing,
  The glory of flowers was her face
And her smile was the smile of the spring.


Madly his blood with a bound
  Leaped from his heart to his brain,
Till his thoughts and his senses were drowned
  In the ache of a longing like pain,
In a hush that was louder than sound.


Then the god, bending his face,
  " Loveliest," said he, " if death
Mocked me with skulls in this place
  And age and spent strength and spent breath,
Yet would I yield to thy grace ;

"Yet would I circle thee, love,
  With these arms which are smoking from wars,
Though the father up-gathered above,
  In his anger, each ocean that roars,
Each boulder the cataracts shove,


"To hurl at me down from his throne,
  Though the flood were as wide as the sky.
Yea, love, I am thine, all thine own,
  Strong as the ocean to lie
Slave to thy bidding alone."


Folds of her vesture fell soft,
  As she lifted her eyes up to his :
"Nay, love, for a man speaketh oft
  In words that are hot as a kiss,
But man's love may be donned and be doft."


"Love would have life for its field—
  Love would have death for its goal :
And the passion of war must yield
  To the passion of love in the soul,
And the eyes that Love kisses are sealed."

"Wouldst thou love if the scorn of the world
  Covered thy head with its briars ;
When, soft as an infant curled
  In its cradle, thou, chained with desires,
Lay helpless when flags were unfurled?"


Fiercely the god's anger broke,
  Fired with the flames in his blood:
"Who careth what words may be spoke ?
  For the feet of this love is a flood,
And its finger the weight of a yoke.


"I bow me, sweet, under its power,
  I, who have stooped to none :
I bring thee my strength for a dower,
  And deeds like the path of the sun :
I am thine for an age or an hour."


Then the moon-lady softly unwound
  The girdle of arms interlaced,
And the gold of her tresses unbound,
  Till it fell from her head to her waist,
And then from her waist to the ground.

" Love, thou art mine, thou art mine,"
  Softly she uttered a spell ;
" Under the froth is the wine,
  Under the ocean is hell,
Over the ocean stars shine.


" Lull him, ye winds of the South,
  Charm him, ye rivers that sing,
Flowers be the kiss on his mouth,
  Let his heart be the heart of the spring,
And his passion the hot summer drouth."


Swiftly extending her hands,
  She made a gold dome of her hair :
Dumb with amazement he stands,
  Till down, without noise in the air,
The moon-car descends to the sands.


He taketh her fingers in his,
  Shorn of his strength and his will ;
His brave heart trembles with bliss  -
  Trembles and will not be still,
Mad with the wine of her kiss.

They mount in the car, and its beams
   Shoot over the sea and the earth,
And clothe in a net-work of dreams
   The mountains where rivers have birth,
And the lakes that are fed by the streams.


Swiftly ascending, the car
   Silvers the clouds in its flight.
Piercing the ether afar
   Up to a bridge out of sight
That skirteth the path of a star.


One end of the bridge lay on land,
   The other hung over the deep ;
It was fashioned of ropes of grey sand,
   And cemented together with sleep,
With its undergirths formed like a hand.


Pleasant the land to the sight,
   Laden with blossoms and trees,
And the grasses to left and to right
   Waved in the wind like the seas,
When the blue day is high in the height.

Under the breezy bowers
    Cushions of moss were laid,
And ever through sultry hours
    Fairy-like fountains played,
Cooling the earth with their showers.


The horizon was crowned with blue hills,
    And woodland and meadowland lay
Lit with the glory which thrills
    Souls in some dreamland way,
Where the nightingales sing to the rills.


Deer and the white kine feed
    On the foam-fretted shores of the lake,
And through many a flowery mead,
    And from many a forest and brake,
The gold birds of paradise speed.


The lissome moon-lady led on
    Up to a bower on a hill
With the flowers at its door rained upon
    By a fountain as constant and still
As the bow in the cloud that has gone.

"O love, thou art weary," she said,
  "Who erst wast so valiant and strong,
And here will I make thee a bed,
  And here will I sing thee a song
To the tune of the leaves overhead.


".And here will thy great strength flow,
  Melted away in the sweet,
Soft touch of ineffable woe,
  Which is heart of the joy made complete,
And the taste of the pleasure we know."


Where the mosses were piled in a heap,
  He laid his giant form down,
And she charmed all his senses to sleep,
  With her hands on his head like a crown,
Till the sound of his breathing was deep.


With a noise like a serpent's hiss,
  The moon-lady bent her head.
And she sucked out his breath with a kiss—
  A kiss that was subtle and dread,
Like the sorrow which lurks in a bliss.

Then she rose and waved her hands
   In circles over the sod,
And her gold hair wove in strands
   Round the limbs of the sleeping god,
With the strength of adamant bands.


She opened the great, clenched fist,
   And softly the lady withdrew,
Was it only a serpent that hissed?
   For her face is transparent as dew,
And her garments are thin as the mist.


Spell-bound on the dreamland floor,
   Chained with the golden hair,
Weak as a babe lay Thor,
   While the fountain played soft in the air,
And the nightingales sang evermore.


Like a babe in its cradle curled,
   He was chained with his chain of desires,
Though they needed his arm in the world,
   For the battle-strife raged, and its fires
And the flags of the gods were unfurled.

Then Odin, the father of Heaven,
　　Called a council of gods on high,
To each was a white cloud given
　　At the foot of his throne in the sky,
And the steps of his throne were seven.


"Children," the father cried,
　　" Lost is the great god Thor,
Lost is the sword at his side,
　　Lost is his arm in the war,
And the fury which all things defied.


" In the heart of a dreamland bower,
　　Sleepeth he under a spell,
For he yielded his strength for an hour,
　　And under the meshes of Hell
He is chained by invincible power.


"None may the meshes unbind ;
　　Strength must return to his will,
And himself must unshackle his mind
　　From the dreams he is dreaming still,
In the moon-lady's tresses entwined.

"Over the mountains the road,
    Dismal and drear to return,
Face it he must with his load,
    Though the underbrakes crackle and burn,
Though the serpent-bites blister and goad.

"Not a mere shadow is sin,
    Clinging like wine to the lip,
To be wiped from the mouth and the chin
    After man taketh a sip;
But a poison that lurketh within.

"The forces that hold back the sea,
    That grapple the earth from beneath,
Are not older than those which decree
    The marriage of sin unto death
In the sinner, whoever he be.

"Who of our numbers will go
    Up to the death-tainted land,
Braving the dangers, and so
    Reaching the heart and the hand
And the form of the god lying low?"

"Sire," answered Balder the fair,
  "Rugged the journey and long,
Manifold dangers are there,
  But my heart and my arms are strong,
And my soul is as pure as the air.


" I will go, for we need him in war,
  And without him we struggle and die :
I will put on the armour he bore
  And gird on his sword to my thigh :
I will sit by and say, ' I am Thor.'


" Perchance when he opens his eyes,
  Shorn of his own armour-plate,
Smitten with rage and surprise,
  Burning with anger and hate,
He will burst from the bed where he lies.


" Swift as the kiss of the fire,
  Knowledge shall flash to his brain,
And the thought of his past self inspire
  His spirit with valour again,
Till he shatter the bonds of desire."

So Balder, the fairest of all,
    And purest of gods by the throne,
Went from the heavenly hall
    Into the darkness alone,
To loosen the god from his thrall.


Black was the charger he rode,
    Winged, and its eye-balls of fire;
From mountain to mountain it trode,
    Spurning the valleys as mire,
Till it sprang into air with its load.


Then swift, with its neck side-curled,
    Half hid in the smoke of its breath,
Upward it bounded, and hurled
    Volleys and splinters of death
From the fire of its hoofs on the world.


The moon-lady leaned from her car
    And beheld the fierce course of the god,
For, as though with the birth of a star,
    A fire track as straight as a rod
Burnt in the heavens afar.

C

Then she trembled and sickened with fear,
  Till her face grew as white as the mist
When at day-dawn the stars disappear,
  And her body did coil and untwist
Like a serpent's folds caught in a weir.


Her heart was a fire that was spent,
  Her lips could not utter a charm,
And she cowered from his sight as he went,
  While Balder flew by without harm,
'Neath the shield of a pure intent.


He came to the moon-lady's bower,
  And girded the sword to his thigh,
And put on the cincture of power,
  Unbound from the god lying by,
Nor waited a day nor an hour:


For, startled, the sleeper awoke,
  Black-visaged, like storm on the skies:
But Balder sat upright, nor spoke,
  Till the flames darted out of Thor's eyes,
And the passionate silence he broke.

"Who is it, when dreaming is o'er,
  Mocks me with helm like to mine,
Ungirding the armour I bore,
  From the sweet silken nets that entwine?"
Quoth Balder, "Behold! I am Thor.


"I am he that was 'Thunderer' called,
  And my fame is as wide as the world;
At my anger the rocks were appalled,
  And the waves of the sea were up-curled,
But now I am weak and enthralled.


"The battle is fierce on the earth,
  While I sit here idle and still;
Unfulfilled are the hopes of my birth,
  For the strength of the mind is the will,
And the will is more potent than girth.


"The foes of the gods wax bold,
  And they mock at the armies of heaven;
At their banquets the story is told—
  'A weak woman's heart hath been given
To Thor, the avenger of old.'

" And the wives as they sit by the cot,
    Sing, 'Sleep, for the god cannot come ;
Sleep, the avenger is not ;
    Hush, let his praises be dumb ;
Hush, let his name be forgot.' "


Then the god, smitten with pain,
    Shamèd and stung to the heart,
Knowing a god's voice again,
    Rending his fetters apart,
Sprang from the moon-lady's chain.


Instantly vanished in night
    Fountains and meadows and streams,
Never a glimmer of light
    Lit up the palace of dreams,
As the god made his way, without sight,


Back to the heavenly shore,
    Over mountain and wild ravine,
Morasses, and seas that roar,
    Till the portals of heaven were seen
And he stood in Valhalla once more.

# THE FEUD.

"I hear a cry from the Sansard cave,
  O mother, will no one hearken?
A cry of the lost, will no one save?
A cry of the dead, though the oceans rave,
And the scream of a gull as he wheels o'er a grave,
  While the shadows darken and darken."


"Oh, hush thee, child, for the night is wet,
  And the cloud-caves split asunder,
With lightning in a jagged fret,
Like the gleam of a salmon in the net,
When the rocks are rich in the red sunset,
  And the stream rolls down in thunder."


"Mother, O mother, a pain at my heart,
  A pang like the pang of dying."
"Oh, hush thee, child, for the wild birds dart
Up and down, and close and part,

Wheeling round where the black cliffs start,
    And the foam at their feet is flying."


"O mother, a strife like the black clouds' strife,
    And a peace that cometh after."
"Hush, child, for peace is the end of life,
And the heart of a maiden finds peace as a wife,
But the sky and the cliffs and the ocean are rife
    With the storm and thunder's laughter."


"Come in, my sons, come in and rest,
    For the shadows darken and darken,
And your sister is pale as the white swan's breast,
And her eyes are fixed and her lips are pressed
In the death of a name ye might have guessed,
    Had ye twain been here to hearken."


"Hush, mother, a corpse lies on the sand,
    And the spray is round it driven,
It lies on its face, and one white hand
Points through the mist on the belt of strand
To where the cliffs of Sansard stand,
    And the ocean's strength is riven."

"Was it God, my sons, who laid him there?
  Or the sea that left him sleeping?"
"Nay, mother, our dirks where his heart was bare,
As swift as the rain through the teeth of the air;
And the foam-fingers play in the Saxon's hair,
  While the tides are round him creeping."


"Oh, curses on you hand and head,
  Like the rains in this wild weather,
The guilt of blood is swift and dread,
Your sister's face is cold and dead,
Ye may not part whom God would wed
  And love hath knit together."

## THE FRENZY OF PROMETHEUS.

THE ocean beats its noontide harmonies
Upon the sunlit lines of cragged coast,
And a wild rhythm pulses through my brain
With pauses and responsive melodies :
And sky and ocean, air and day and night
Topple and reel upon my burning blood,
Run to and fro, whirl round and round and round,
Till, lo! the cosmic madness breathes a strain
Of perfect music through the universe.
I hear it with my ears, eyes, hands and feet,
I drink it with my breath, my skin sucks in
At every fevered pore fine threads of sound,
Which plunge vibrations of the wind-swept harp
Of earth and heaven deep into my soul,
Till each sense kindles with a freshened life,
And thoughts arise which bring me ease from pain.

O peace, sweet peace! I melt and ebb away,
On softened rocks outstretch relaxèd limbs,

With half-shut eyes deliciously enthralled.
What passion, what delight, what ecstasies !
Joy fills my veins with rivers of excess :
I rave, I quiver, as with languid eyes
I see the hot air dance upon the rocks,
And sky, sea, headlands blend in murmurous haze.


Now grander, with the organ's bass that rolls
The under-world in darkness through despair
Of any day-dawn on its inky skies,
The music rolls around me, and above
From shattered cliffs, from booming caverns' mouths,
Pierced by the arrow-screams of frightened gulls.
Now strength, subdued, but waxing more and more,
Reanimates my limbs : I feel my power
Full as the flooding ocean, or the force
Which grinds the glaciers on their boulder feet.
My hands could pluck up mountains by the roots,
My arm could hurl back ocean from the shore
To wallow in his frothy bed.   What hate ! what scorn
What limitless imaginations stretch
And burst my mind immense : I stand apart,
I am alone, all-glorious, supreme :

My huge form like a shadow sits and broods
Upon the globe, gigantic, like the shade
Eclipsing moons.   With bowed head on my hand
In gloom excessive, now, behold, I see
Beneath my feet the stream of human life
The sad procession of humanity.


They come, the sons of Hellas, beautiful,
Swift-minded, lithe, with luscious, laughing lips,
That suck delight from every tree of life :
Born of the sunshine, winds and sounding sea.
They pass, and, lo, a mightier nation moves
In stern battalions trampling forests down,
Cleaving the mountains, paving desert lands
With bones that e'en when bleaching face the foe,
Welding soft outskirt nations into iron,
An iron hand to grasp and hold the world.


Now dust, like smoke, from Asia's central steppes,
Darkens the rigid white of mountain peaks,
And the plains bristle with the Tartar hordes,
Suckled of mares, flat-faced, implacable,

Deadly in war, revengeful, treacherous,
Brown as the craggy glens of Caucasus.
They pass, and nations pass, and like a dream
A throne emerges from the western sea,
The latest empire of a dying world.
E'en as I look its splendour melts away,
And round me, gathering volume, music rolls,
Till sinews crack and eyes are blind with power,
Till struggles, battles mixed with smoke and blood,
Men, nations, life and death, and desolate cries,
Melt in the inner pulses in my ears
And a wild tempest blows the daylight out.


And now I am alone beneath the stars,
Alone, in infinite silence.   Am I God,
That I am so supreme?   Whence is this power?
Cannot my will repeople these waste lands?
I cry aloud, the vault of space resounds,
And hollow-sounding echoes, from the stars
Rebounding, shake the earth and crinkle up
The sea in million furrows.   Lo, the stars
Now fade, the sun arises, it is day,
Half day, half night ; the sun hath lost his strength,

I am his equal, nay I am his king !
I rise and move across the earth, the seas
Have vanished, and I tread their empty beds,
And crush down continents of powdered bones.


O great light, late supreme, what need of thee ?
For all are dead, men, nations, life and death,
And God is dead and here alone am I—
I, with strong hands to pluck thee from thy course,
Boundless in passions, will, omnipotent.
The impulses concentre in my heart
Which erstwhile shook the universe.   O Sun,
Acknowledge now thy king, put down thy head
Beneath my feet, and lift me higher still
To regions that out-top the adoring spheres,
And bask in primal thought, too vast to shape
Into similitude of earthly things.


I would have all, know all.   I thirst and pant
And hunger for the universe.   Now from the earth,
Beneath thy rays, O Sun, the steams arise,
Sheeting the world's dead face in film of cloud,
The voices of the dead.   Peace, let me be.

Go on thy way, spent power, leave me here
To reign in silence, rave and scorn and hate,
To glory in my strength, tear down the skies,
Trample the crumbling mountains under foot,
Laugh at the tingling stars, burn with desire
Unconquerable, till the universe
Is shattered at the core, its splinters flung
By force centrifugal beyond the light,
Until the spent stars from their orbits reel,
And, hissing down the flaming steeps of space,
With voice of fire proclaim me God alone.

# NATURA VICTRIX.

On the crag I sat in wonder,
Stars above me, forests under :
   Through the valleys came and went
   Tempest forces never spent,
And the gorge sent up the thunder
   Of the stream within it pent.

Round me with majestic bearing
Stood the giant mountains, wearing
   Helmets of eternal snows,
   Cleft by nature's labour throes—
Monster faces mutely staring
   Upward into God's repose.

At my feet in desolation
Swayed the pines, a shadowy nation,
   Round the woodlake deep and dread,
   Round the river glacier-fed,

Where a ghostly undulation
  Shakes its subterranean bed.


And I cried, " O wildernesses !
Mountains ! which the wind caresses,
  In a savage love sublime,
  Through the bounds of space and time,
All your moods and deep distresses
  Roll around me like a chime.


" Lo, I hear the mighty chorus
Of the elements that bore us
  Down the course of nature's stream,
  Onward in a haunted dream
Towards the darkness, where before us
  Time and death forgotten seem.


" Now behold the links of lightning
Round the neck of storm-god tightening,
  Madden him with rage and shame
  Till he smites the earth with flame,
In the darkening and the brightening
  Of the clouds on which he came.

" Nature ! at whose will are driven
Tides of ocean, winds of heaven,
    Thou who rulest near and far
    Forces grappling sun and star,
Is to thee the knowledge given
    Whence these came and what they are?


" Is thy calm the calm of knowing
Whence the force is, whither going ?
    Is it but the blank despair
    Of the wrecked, who does not care
Out at sea what wind is blowing
    To the death that waits him there ?


" Mother Nature, stern aggressor,
Of thy child the mind-possessor,
    Thou art in us like a flood,
    Welling through our thought and blood—
Force evolving great from lesser,
    As the blossom from the bud.


" Yea, I love thy fixed, enduring
Times and seasons, life procuring

From abysmal heart of thine ;
And my spirit would resign
All its dreams and hopes alluring
With thy spirit to combine.


" Would that I, amid the splendour
Of the thunder-blasts, could render
Back the dismal dole of birth,
Fusing soul clouds in the girth
Of thy rock breasts, or the tender
Green of everlasting earth.


" Haply, when the scud was flying
And the lurid daylight dying
Through the rain-smoke on the sea,
Thoughtless, painless, one with thee,
I, in perfect bondage lying,
Should forever thus be free.


" Mighty spirits, who have striven
Up life's ladder-rounds to heaven,
Or ye freighted ones who fell
On the poppy slopes of hell,

D

When the soul was led or driven,
 Knew ye not who wrought the spell?


" Understood not each his brother
From the features of our mother
 Stamped on every human face?
 Did not earth, man's dwelling place,
Draw ye to her as no other,
 With a stronger bond than grace?


" Tempest hands the forests rending,
Placid stars the night attending,
 Mountains, storm-clouds, land and sea,
 Nature!—make me one with thee:
From my soul its pinions rending,
 Chain me to thy liberty.


" Hark! the foot of death is nearing,
And my spirit aches with fearing,
 Hear me, mother, hear my cry,
 Merge me in the harmony
Of thy voice which stars are hearing
Wonder-stricken in the sky.

" Mother, will no sorrow move thee?
Does the silence heartless prove thee?
   Thou who from the rocks and rain
   Mad'st this soul, take back again
What thy fingers wrought to love thee
   Through the furnace of its pain.

" Giant boulders, roll beside me,
Tangled ferns, bow down and hide me,
   Hide me from the face of death :
   Or, great Nature, on thy breath
Send some mighty words to guide me,
   Till the demon vanisheth."

Then as sweet as organ playing,
Came a voice, my fears allaying,
   From the mountains and the sea,
   "Wouldst thou, soul, be one with me,
In thy might the slayer slaying?
   Wrestle not with what must be."

Heart and spirit in devotion,
Vibrant with divine emotion,

Bowed before that mighty sound,
And amid the dark around
Quaffed the strength of land and ocean
In a sacrament profound.

Then I burst my bonds asunder,
And my voice rose in the thunder
With a full and powerful breath,
Strong for what great nature saith,
And I bade the stars in wonder
See me slay the slayer—death.

# THE ABBOT.

A WANING moon was in the sky
And many a still cloud floated by,
With outline dark the abbey stood
    Fronting a line of wood.

With bowed head on the chapel stone
The Abbot knelt for hours alone,
While round him coloured moonbeams threw
    Rose-work of richest hue.

A tiny altar-lamp burnt dim,
And lit the sculptured seraphim
Which fringed the choir with faces bent
    Before the Sacrament.

The place was still as in a dream,
So very still, the ear did seem
To catch the voice of years gone by,
    And long dead harmony.

The abbey clock above struck three,
The Abbot rose from bended knee,
His face was greyer than the stone,
 His eyes were woe-begone.

He passed into the cloister dim,
The night-air brought no balm to him,
What anguish made his senses reel,
 Christ could not heal?

He entered at an iron grate,
The halls within were desolate;
Like one who waketh from a spell,
 He halted at a cell.

Therein upon a pallet bed,
With bars of moonlight on his head,
While winds through ivied mullions creep,
 A fair-haired boy did sleep.

Outside an owl did hoot and call
And drown the Abbot's light foot-fall,
But rustle of those garments cere
 In dreams the boy did hear.

"Hush, boy, 'tis I," the Abbot said,
"Thy pure soul to the rescued dead
Shall bear my message; life is past,
    Hell's meshes hold me fast.

"Was thy sleep sweet? my sleep is o'er,
One speaks to thee who never more
Shall look on man (God send us grace),
    Nor ever see God's face."

The boy through fear sat bolt upright
In tongueless terror, for moonlight
Smote slanting on the face and eye,
    Which worked convulsively.

"One burden, boy, a weight of years,
Full to the brim of hopeless tears,
Hath crushed me, bearing round my brain
    The double brand of Cain.

"Thy life and hopes are all before,
And mine are passed for evermore;
My secret in the years to come
    Remember, but be dumb.

"O God, my heart beats loud within,
I slew my brother in mortal sin,
I stabbed him twice, not knowing, to free
    A maiden's chastity."


The Abbot stood erect and tall,
His shadow fell along the wall,—
God save him, as if seeking grace,
    He hid his cowlèd face.


"A black snake slipt across my feet,
Above bare boughs did part and meet,
There was a motion in the air
    And eyes watched everywhere.


"The deed was done in distant lands,
But his blood dabbled these same hands,
And under trees where pale stars shine
    His eyes looked into mine.


"One look from those dead eyes of his,
And love rushed back to him; was this
The climax of his life who seemed
    The king my boyhood dreamed?

"Shall sin and shall not love endure?
Love grounded in the past and pure,
Man's love for man, for angels fit,
    Could one act shatter it?"

The boy sat upright, pale as death,
A numbness stole away his breath,
The fascination of the eye,
    Which moved convulsively.

" I fled at sunrise down the bay
To where a mystic island lay,
Dazed with the cloudless arch of sky
    And waves' monotony.

" And here a convent open stood,
Where monks sought peace in solitude ;
I entered with the rest to hide
    Within the Crucified.

" I told my woe to one : he said,—
' Under thy feet, and overhead,
And all around is God.  To-night,
    Keep vigil, pray for light.'

"That night in cave-shrine, visions three
God and the Virgin sent to me ;
Four angels fenced the cavern's mouth
　　With locked wings, north and south.

"Thrice darkness fell, and thrice I lay
Low-poised above a sea, no day
Lit up its shoreless waves, no night
　　Shut distance from the sight.

"No fish leaped up, no God looked down,
No sound there was, I strove to drown,—
Ere waves were touched a wind did spring,
　　And bore me on its wing.

"My blood stood still and thick as ice,
And thought held thought, as in a vice,
The ages died, no death did bless
　　The death of nothingness.

"Each time the soul did undergo
The torture of a separate woe,
The demon fangs insatiate,
　　Of doubt, despair and hate.

" I woke and told the monk my dreams ;
His voice was sad, he said, ' Meseems
No part one slain in his soul's blood
　　Shall have in Holy Rood.


" ' But brother,' said the agèd man,
' God works by many a diverse plan,
And once vicarious agony
　　Saved souls on Calvary.


" ' I know not but, with God in heaven,
Some grace to lost souls may be given ;
By fasts and scourgings, prayers and pains,
　　Loose thou thy brother's chains.'


" Yea, boy, have I not prayed to Heaven ?
Has not life spoilt with bitter leaven
And fasts and scourgings, night and day,
　　The blood-guilt burnt away ?


" But ever from the throat of hell
There booms a fearful passing bell
Of one, once slain in his soul's blood,
　　Cast out from Holy Rood.

"The passions of the full-grown man
Concentre where his life began:
The boy's love is not manifold,
    It grips with single hold.

"The boyhood's love is part of us,
No power can wrench it out, and thus
Love chained me to him in the gloom,
    And I had wrought his doom.

"The thing was with me day by day,
And all my thinking underlay;
And even through hours when I forgot,
    Ached as a canker spot.

"My food was ashes in my mouth,
My very soul was seared with drouth,
I banished thought, the struggle vain
    Brought back the thought again.

"The saints and angels held aloof,
My prayers fell back from chapel roof,
They had no lightness to ascend
    Where earth and heaven blend.

" The stars did mock me with their peace,
The seasons brought me no release,
Despair and anguish like a sea
 And pain were under me.


" And year by year more pains I gave,
Till life became a living grave,
Till, like the lost behind hell's gate,
 My soul was desolate."


Outside, an owl did hoot and call,
But in the abbey silence all ;
The Abbot's voice had hollow sound,
 As if from underground.


" Hush, boy, the fiend came yesternight."
The Abbot smiled—a gruesome sight,
That smiling face in moonlight wan,
 With eyes so woe-begone—


" The fiend came yesternight to ask
The utmost deed that life can task,
A soul by self-death given to win
 Another's soul from sin."

So fearful was the story told,
The boy's teeth chattered as with cold,
He saw no leaf-shapes on the floor,
    He heard no bell ring four.

" To-night with head on chapel stone,
I prayed to Him who did atone,
Till blood-sweat ran, as down His face
    It ran in garden-place.

" 'Tis done, the earthly fight is o'er,
My soul is dark for evermore,
I am the fiend's, hark ! hear him call—
    He holds a soul in thrall.

" I know not if the spirit breath,
Meets spirit on the road of death,
Or falleth like a thin, white thread
    Among the under dead.

" I know not whether, passing by,
One rapid moment, he and I,
His face upturned to coming crown,
    Mine anguished, bending down,

"Shall then know all : but boy, when near
Thy feet approach where tier on tier,
God's minstrels face the Trinity,
    In that place made for me,

" But mine no longer, seek thou there
One with thine eyes and golden hair,
Gold as his broidered vesture is,
    And say whose soul won his.

" Perchance, though there no sorrow dims,
The tears will mount to his eyes' brims,
And I shall live, his sweetest thought,
    For what my love hath wrought.

" Again the demon calls, I come.
See, pure boy, let thy lips be dumb,
One last atonement lifts to-night
    A lost soul into light."

He kissed the boy upon the brow :
" Yea, very like to him art thou,
When we sat pure on mother's knee,
    Farewell, eternally."

The Abbot passed into the gloom,
The moonlight flooded all the room.
The boy sat stark from hour to hour,
    Chained by unearthly power.

But lo, when, in the matin time,
The bells rang out the hour of prime,
From cloistered aisle and chapel stair
    A wild cry rent the air.

Not yet quite cold, dead in his blood,
With face averted from the Rood,
The Abbot lay on chapel stone,
    His eyes still woe-begone.

No bell was rung, no mass was said,
They buried the dishonoured dead
Out in the road which crossed the wood,
    In dark and solitude.

They marked the spot with never a stone,
Tree-shadows fell on it alone,
And moss and vines and thin wood grass
    Grew where no feet would pass.

Nathless, it seemed to one fair boy,
The birds did sing with fuller joy,
And angels swung wood incense faint,
    As round the grave of saint.

The tiny altar-lamp burnt dim,
And lit the sculptured seraphim,
And tombs where monks in garments cere
    Were gathered year by year.

But when an old monk came to die,
He spake thus to those standing by :
" Out in that spot my grave be set,
    Marked by wood violet.

" No man can judge another's sin,
God only sees without and in,
Wherefore, my brethren, be ye kind,
    That was our Master's mind.

" For many are crowned as saints by God
Whose graves unheeding feet have trod ;
Man judges by the outer life,
    God by the inner strife.

E

"Out there the forest tree-roots creep
Round one sad heart's forgotten sleep,
A heart which broke in giving all
  To save a soul from thrall."

# DION.

## A POEM.

### ARGUMENT.

Dion, of Syracuse (408 353 B.C.), philosopher,
was a near relative, through his wife Arete, of the
tyrant Dionysius the Second, by whom he was
banished. He took up his residence at Athens, but
on hearing that the tyrant had seized his son and
given Arete in marriage to another, with a small and
faithful force he returned to Syracuse, captured the
place and drove Dionysius into Ortygia, a fortress
within the city walls. As soon as their oppression
was relieved, the suspicious Syracusans began to fear
the power of Dion, although he had nobly refused to
make concessions to Dionysius when urged thereto
by the passionate appeals of Arete and her son, held
captive in Ortygia. On hearing of a plot formed
against him among the citizens, by Heracleides, without taking revenge on the thankless city, Dion withdrew to Leontini, but only to be speedily recalled to
rescue the people a second time from the ravages of
Dionysius, who had charged out upon the town as
soon as Dion had withdrawn. Again Dion returned
to Syracuse, and this time succeeded in routing the
tyrant from his stronghold and restoring peace. With

a magnanimity equal to his valour he pardoned Heracleides and his confreres.    On breaking into the
deserted fortress at the head of his troops, Dion, after
years of separation, found his wife Arete.    Dion
naturally succeeded to the throne of the deposed
monarch, but his reforms and the severity of his
manners and rule rendered him unpopular with his
fickle fellow-townsmen, and plots were formed for his
assassination.    He scorned to take precautions against
attack, and so fell a victim to his valour.    He was
surrounded on the day of the festival of the Koreia,
in his apartment in the palace, by a band of youths
of distinguished muscular strength, who endeavoured
to throw and strangle him.    But the old warrior
proving too strong for them, they were obliged to
send out one of their number through a back door to
procure a sword.    With this, Dion, a man in many
ways too great for his age and circumstances, was
despatched.


Pray youths, what urgent business claims our ear
On this high feast when all keep holiday?
Already do the gay-decked barges move
Across the harbour to the sacred grove,
And shouts and music reach us even here,
Where through the balustrades the dancing sea
Marbles this chamber with reflected lights.
What !   Is it treason?   Ye have come to slay,
I read your purpose right.   The palace guards

Have been secured and all retreat cut off,
And I am at your mercy.   It is well.
So often have I met death face to face,
His eyes now wear the welcome of a friend's.
Is it for hate of Dion, or for gold,
Ye come to stain your honour with my blood ?
And think ye I shall kneel and fawn on you,
And cry for mercy with a woman's shrieks ?
Though me, like some old lion in his den,
Fate, stratagems, not ye, have tracked to death.
The lion is old, but all his teeth are sound.
What ! Ye would seize me ?  There, I shake you off.
Ye did not deem these withered arms so strong
That ye five cubs could thus be kept at bay,
Despite your claws, and fury, and fierce barks.
But I am Dion—Dion, Plato's friend,
And I have faced the rain of human blood,
The lightning of the sword-strokes on my helm,
The thunder of on-rushing cavalry,
When ye were sucking babies at the breast.
And think ye I am one whom ye can slay
By throttling, as an outcast slays her child,
Pinching the life out of its tiny throat?
Not this shall be my death, for I am royal,

And I must royally die.   Go fetch a sword
And I shall wed it nobly like a king.

I brought you manhood with my conquering arm,
I offered Syracuse a way to fame.
I could have made our city reign as queen,
With her dominion founded in the sea,
Cemented with wise bands of equal laws,
A constitution wrought by sober minds,
Expanding with its growth, yet ye would not,
But mewed and babbled, cried and sulked again,
Like children that will quarrel for a coin
And yet its value know not.   I am king.
Beyond this honour, if it honour be,
To sit enthroned above so base a herd,—
A king of mine own self.   My thoughts are matched
With those of gods, I have no kin with you.
Go publish my last words when I am dead,
And sting the city's heart with them.   Say, " Thus,
O men of Syracuse, thus Dion spake,
Falling upon the threshold of his death,
With face turned back, eyes fixed, and cheek
        unblanched,
For one last moment, at the braying mob,

Ere into dark he passed to meet his peers,
The gods and heroes of the nether world."
Yea, tell the foolish rabble, " Dion sends
His love and duty, as a warrior should,
Unto the sweet earth of his native town,
Soon to be watered with his warmest blood.
He loved her pleasant streets, her golden air,
The circle of her hills, her sapphire sea,
And he loved once, and loved unto his death,
The poor, half-brutal thing her mob became
Under the heel of tyrants ; had he not,
He might have finished out his course of days
And died among the pillows on his bed.
But he so loved his Syracuse that she,
Grown sick of his great heart, let out its red
Upon the pebbles of her streets, and cried,
' Mine own hands slew him, for he loved too much.'

" Too much, ay, at her piteous call he came
And gripped the tyrant's heel upon your neck,
And overthrew him, bidding you uprise.
And when your silly fathers feared his strength,
And set their murderous snares around his path,
The sword he drew for her, for her he sheathed,

Disdaining as a warrior to be wroth
At the snake's use of its recovered power
To sting the breast that warmed it back to life ;
And he whose word could then have crushed the town
Into a shapeless ruin at his feet,
Led off to Leontini all his men,
Who, had ye slain him, would upon the ground
Have heaped your bodies for his funeral pyre ;
And who, with eyes that cursed her very stones,
Left Syracuse unharmed, at his command.
Yet on the morrow in your new distress
Ye were not loth to send with craven haste
Your weeping envoys fawning at his feet
And crying, 'Come and save us ; oh, forget,
Great Dion, how we wronged thee, come again,
Yet this once more, and save our Syracuse.'

" 'There are no depths in ocean, earth or sky
So deep as Dion's pride : there is no force
Commensurate with the scorn which curled his lip
In detestation of the fickle world,
Before he plunged forever down death's gulf.
So proud was he, that he despised success,
His manhood was the crown his spirit wore.

His stern heart felt no pulse of arrogant joy
When charging foremost on the routed ranks
Of Dionysius in precipitous flight ;
Nor when, as conqueror, up the city's hill
The wild mob bore him with their loud acclaims,
And women from the house-roofs hailed him king,
And shrilled his praises out to the great deep.
But he was proud, as might some god be proud,
At his self-conquest, when for mercy sued
False Heracleides, whose perfidious plot
To overthrow him well-nigh wrought your doom.
Ye saw the traitor kneel, ye heard his words,
How his swift tongue did hide the poisoned fangs.
But when all voices shouted, ' Let him die,'
The one most wronged obeyed that inner voice
Which bade him spare a fallen enemy.
And stooping down, he raised and pardoned him,
Well knowing as ye the baseness of the man,
But being too great for meanness like revenge.

" Had Dion not been proud, O Syracuse,
He might have told such tale of woes endured
As would, like some moist south-wind after frost,
Have made your very walls and porticos

Run down with tears of silent sympathy.
Ye thought that day he read to you unmoved
The letter that his own son wrote to him
In his young blood, sobbed out with broken cries,
While Dionysius pressed the red-hot irons
Close on his slim boy's back, that he was stone,
Inhuman, or if human, weak like you,
And would with treason buy him from his chains.
Nay, but ye knew not how his father's heart
Burnt with the fury of the molten sun,
And how the ashes of his being choked
The steadfast voice which cried, 'I will not yield,
I will not wrong my blood with treachery
To what is right—the gods deliver him.'

" 'Twas well ye marked him not that other day
When he broke first into the citadel
Deserted by the tyrant, and there found,
Whiter, more stone-like than the marble shaft
'Gainst which she crouched from him in speechless fear,
His wife, his long-lost Arete, and went
And drew her white hands from her face and said,
'My wife, my own, thy Dion comes again,
And his great love doth wash thy body clean

From sins forced on thee, which were not thine own.'
For as she rose and clung about his neck,
Panting and quivering like a hunted fawn,
She downward bent her face in guileless shame
And told him, with her cheek against his breast,
How through those years of captive misery
She, like a priestess, had in secret shrine
Of wedded heart kept ever bright and pure
The vestal flame of her great love for him.
'Twas well ye marked not, Syracusan men,
How unlike stone was Dion then, how fell
His woman's tears upon her woman's hair.
'Twas well ye heard not what his heart pulsed out,
Without one word, into her tight-pressed ear,
Else might ye and your wives have called him weak,
When ye had seen that inner self laid bare
Which he forsook to serve his native land."

A strong tree which has braved a thousand storms
May totter in the wind which brings its fall,
So now methinks my pride is dying down
When thus I talk before my funeral
Of all the love, hate, duty, self-restraint,
Ingratitude and anguish, which have graved

And scarred old Dion as he is to-day,
With all his years gone by and all his deeds.

And now, eternal gods, I come to you
Through death, with calm, irrevocable tread.
Farewell, life's toilsome warfare.   Like a king,
Great gods, receive me into bliss or woe,
Whiche'er your land affordeth ; set my throne
Among the company of those who strove
To mount by inner conquest, not by blood :
And who accept and quaff with equal mind
Pleasure or pain, defeat or victory.
I care not to be highest, only peer
Of all the great who are in-gathered there :
If needs my rank be blazoned on my throne,
Inscribe it, " Dion, Tyrant of Himself."

Ha ! ye have found a sword : 'tis well, for now
I shall lie down to sleep as soldier should,
Wounded in front and by a soldier's blade.
O Syracuse, I thought to carve a rock
Rough and unhewn into a perfect shape ;
But lo ! 'twas only clay wherewith I wrought,
And every wind and rain did melt you down

Into the common mud which tyrants love
To smooth into an easy path to power.

Here, youths, I do not flinch, behold my breast,
Shaggy, like front of lion, streaked with grey.
It is your glory to anticipate
Time's tardy slaughter.  Come, which will be great
And first to make himself a name and steep
His weakling hands in Dion's royal blood?
Pray you be quick, I do not fear the pain,
But would quit life.  Here is my naked heart :
It knocks against the edges of this rib,
But yet not faster than its wont.  Come, youths,
Put the sword here and drive it quickly home,
And fix your eyes upon me as I fall,
And mark ye well the grandeur of my death.
For nothing but the red flood bursting forth,
No cry, no groan, no movement of the face,
Shall tell you that ye have not slain a god.
Then draw the blade out blunted where it met
The tempered edge of my self-mastering will,
And bear the crimsoned trophy through the streets,
And show it to the wondering citizens :
That men may know and tell in aftertimes
How Dion lived and died for Syracuse.

# LOVE SLIGHTED.

Love built a chamber in my heart,
  A daintier ne'er was seen,
'Twas filled with books and gems of art,
And all that makes a lover's part
  True homage to his Queen.

The ceiling was of silver bright
  That showed the floor below ;
The walls were hung with silk so white
That e'en the mirror was to sight
  A slope of driven snow.

Then Love threw open wide the door,
  And sang, as in a dream,
A song as sweet as bird can pour
Above the sunlight-marbled floor
  Of some clear forest stream.

He sang of youth that ne'er grows old,
   Of flowers that ne'er decay,
Of wine whose sweetness is not told,
Of honour bright, and courage bold,
   And faith more fair than they.


And many a maiden passed me by,
   Though some would hear and start,
But thought the singing was so high,
It came from somewhere in the sky,
   And not from my poor heart.


So years have come and years have flown
   Adown the sunset hill,
But Love still sits and sings alone,
And, though his voice has sweeter grown,
   My heart is empty still.

# ANDANTE.

THE days and weeks are going, love,
  The years roll on apace,
And the hand of time is showing, love,
  In the care lines on thy face ;

But the tie that bound our hearts, love,
  In the morning's golden haze,
Is a tie that never parts, love,
  With the passing of the days.

For though Death's arm be strong, love,
  Our love its light will shed,
And like a glorious song, love,
  Will live when Death is dead.

## SORROW'S WAKING.

Once a maiden,
Heavy-laden,
Sought to borrow
Sleep from sorrow.

Sweet the taking,
But the waking
In the numbness
And the dumbness
Of the day-dawn,
With the grey lawn
Softly plaining
In the raining,
And the meadows
Hid in shadows,
Was more dreary
Than the weary
Mounds which sever
Hearts forever,
Where Death's reaping
Leaves man sleeping
In God's keeping.

# ON AN OLD VENETIAN PORTRAIT.

THE features loom out of the darkness
    As brown as an ancient scroll,
But the eyes gleam on with the fire that shone
    In the dead man's living soul.

He is clad in a cardinal's mantle,
    And he wears the cap of state,
But his lip is curled in a sneer at the world,
    And his glance is full of hate.

Old age has just touched with its winter
    The hair on his lip and chin,
He stooped, no doubt, as he walked about,
    And the blood in his veins was thin.

His date and his title I know not,
    But I know that the man is there,
As cruel and cold as in days of old,
    When he schemed for the Pontiff's chair.

*He* never could get into Heaven,
   Though his lands were all given to pay
For prayers to be said on behalf of the dead
   From now till the judgment day.

His palace, his statues, and pictures
   Were Heaven, at least for a time,
And now he is " Where ? " —why an ornament
     there
   On my wall, and I think him sublime.

For the gold of another sunset
   Falls over him even now,
And it deepens the red of the cap on his head,
   And it brings out the lines on his brow.

The ages have died into silence,
   And men have forgotten his tomb,
But he still sits there in his cardinal's chair,
   And he watches me now in the gloom.

## OLD LETTERS.

THE house was silent, and the light
　　Was fading from the western glow :
I read, till tears had dimmed my sight,
　　Some letters written long ago.

The voices that have passed away,
　　The faces that have turned to mould,
Were round me in the room to-day,
　　And laughed and chatted as of old.

The thoughts that youth was wont to think,
　　The hopes now dead for evermore,
Came from the lines of faded ink,
　　As sweet and earnest as of yore.

I laid the letters by and dreamed
　　The dear dead past to life again :
The present and its purpose seemed
　　A fading vision full of pain.

Then, with a sudden shout of glee,
    The children burst into the room,
Their little faces were to me
    As sunrise in the cloud of gloom.

The world was full of meaning still,
    For love will live though loved ones die ;
I turned upon life's darkened hill
    And gloried in the morning sky.

## VAN ELSEN.

God spake three times and saved Van Elsen's soul ;
He spake by sickness first and made him whole ;
    Van Elsen heard Him not,
    Or soon forgot.

God spake to him by wealth, the world outpoured
Its treasures at his feet, and called him Lord :
    Van Elsen's heart grew fat
    And proud thereat.

God spake the third time when the great world smiled,
And in the sunshine slew his little child :
    Van Elsen like a tree
    Fell hopelessly.

Then in the darkness came a voice which said,
"As thy heart bleedeth, so my heart hath bled,
    As I have need of thee,
    Thou needest me."

That night Van Elsen kissed the baby feet,
And kneeling by the narrow winding sheet,
    Praised Him with fervent breath
    Who conquered death.

# IN MEOMRIAM.

JAMES WILLIAM WILLIAMS, LORD BISHOP OF QUEBEC,
DIED APRIL 20TH, 1892, AGED 66 YEARS.

To those found faithful, oft the call to rest
Comes in the glory of the later noon,
Ere evening falls and with declining day
The mind has darkened and work lost its zest.
So now, though first our sad hearts cried " Too soon,"
We see God's angel did in heavenly way
His finished work and Master's love attest.
And now he wins, withdrawn from human eye,
A good man's two-fold immortality,
To live forever near the Master's throne,
And here, in lives made better by his own.

## THE EVERLASTING FATHER.

Thou whose face is as the lightning and whose
    chariot as the sun,
Unto whom a thousand ages in their passing are as
    one,
All our worlds and mighty systems are but tiny grains
    of sand,
Held above the gulfs of chaos in the hollow of Thy
    hand.

Yea, we see Thy power about us, and we feel its
    volumes roll
Through the torrent of our passions and the stillness
    of the soul,
Where its visions light the darkness till the dawn that
    is to be,
Like the long auroral splendours on a silent polar sea.

Then uplift us, great Creator, to communion with
    Thy will,
Crush our puny heart-rebellions, make our baser
    cravings still.
Thou whose fingers through the ages wrought with
    fire the soul of man,
Blend it more and more forever with the purpose of
    Thy plan.

Speak, O Lord, in voice of thunder, show Thy foot-
    steps on the deep,
Pour Thy sunshine from the heavens on the blinded
    eyes that weep,
Till the harmonies of nature and exalted human love
Make the universe a mirror of the glorious God
    above.

# THE STING OF DEATH.

" Is Sin, then, fair ? "
  Nay, love, come now
Put back the hair
  From his sunny brow :
See, here, blood-red
 Across his head
A brand is set,
The word—" Regret."

" Is Sin so fleet
  That while he stays
Our hands and feet
  May go his ways ? "
Nay, love, his breath
Clings round like death,
He slakes desire
With liquid fire.

" Is Sin Death's sting ? "
  Ay, sure he is,
His golden wing
  Darkens man's bliss :
And when Death comes,
Sin sits and hums
A chaunt of fears
Into man's ears.

" How slayeth Sin ? "
  First, God is hid,
And the heart within
  By its own self chid :
Then the maddened brain
Is scourged by pain
To sin as before
And more and more,
  For evermore.

## TE JUDICE.

Dost thou deem that thyself
  Art as white from sin
As a platter of delf,
  Outside and in?
When thine eyes behold
  Christ's kind face lean
From His throne of gold
To test what is told
  Of the life that hath been,
Like a leper of old,
  Thou wilt cry, "Unclean!
  Unclean!  Unclean!"

And thinkest thou this—
  That thou judgest aright
Thy heart as it is
  In God's and man's sight?

Fool, take up thy light,
And descend the stair steep
To thy heart's dungeons deep,
And search them and sweep
  Till their ghosts are unmasked ;
Else when judgment is come
Thou wilt stand stark and dumb
  At the first question asked.

## THE TWO MISTRESSES.

Ah, woe is me, my heart's in sorry plight,
Enamoured equally of Wrong and Right ;
    Right hath the sweeter grace,
    But Wrong the prettier face :
Ah, woe is me, my heart's in sorry plight.

And Right is jealous that I let Wrong stay ;
Yet Wrong seems sweeter when I turn away.
    Right sober is, like Truth,
    But Wrong is in her youth ;
So Right is jealous that I let Wrong stay.

When I am happy, left alone with Right,
Then Wrong flits by and puts her out of sight ;
    I follow and I fret,
    And once again forget
That I am happy, left alone with Right.

Ah, God ! do Thou have pity on my heart !
A puppet blind am I, take Thou my part !
    Chasten my wandering love,
    Set it on things above :
Ah, God ! do Thou take pity on my heart !

## IN THE WOODS.

THIS is God's house—the blue sky is the ceiling,
 This wood the soft green carpet for His feet,
Those hills His stairs, down which the brooks come
  stealing,
 With baby laughter making earth more sweet.

And here His friends come, clouds and soft winds
  sighing,
 And little birds whose throats pour forth their love,
And spring and summer, and the white snow lying
 Pencilled with shadows of bare boughs above.

And here come sunbeams through the green leaves
  straying,
 And shadows from the storm-clouds overdrawn,
And warm, hushed nights, when mother earth is
  praying
 So late that her moon-candle burns till dawn.

Sweet house of God, sweet earth so full of pleasure,
 I enter at thy gates in storm or calm :
And every sunbeam is a joy and treasure,
 And every cloud a solace and a balm.

# CALVARY.

O sorrowful heart of humanity, foiled in thy fight
for dominion,
   Bowed with the burden of emptiness, blackened
   with passion and woe ;
Here is a faith that will bear thee on waft of
omnipotent pinion,
   Up to the heaven of victory, there to be known
   and to know.


Here is the vision of Calvary, crowned with the
world's revelation,
   Throned in the grandeur of gloom and the
   thunders that quicken the dead ;
A meteor of hope in the darkness shines forth like
a new constellation,
   Dividing the night of our sorrow, revealing a path
   as we tread.

Now are the portals of death by the feet of the
    Conqueror entered ;
  Flames of the sun in his setting roll over the city
    of doom,
And robe in imperial purple the Body triumphantly
    centred,
  Naked and white between thieves and 'mid ghosts
    that have crept from the tomb.


O Soul, that art lost in immensity, craving for light
    and despairing,
  Here is the hand of the Crucified, pulses of love in
    its veins,
Human as ours in its touch, with the sinews of Deity
    bearing
  The zones of the pendulous planets, the weight of
    the winds and the rains.


Here in the Heart of the Crucified, find thee a refuge
    and hiding,
  Love at the core of the universe, guidance and
    peace in the night ;

G

Centuries pass like a flood, but the Rock of our
    Strength is abiding,
  Grounded in depths of eternity, girt with a mantle
    of light.


Lo, as we wonder and worship, the night of the
    doubts that conceal Him,
  Rolls from the face of the dawn till His rays through
    the cloud-fissures slope ;
Vapours that hid are condensed to the dews of His
    grace that reveal Him,
  And shine with His light on the hills as we mount
    in the splendour of hope.

## AT LAUDS.

'Tis sweet to wake before the dawn,
  When all the cocks are crowing,
And from my window on the lawn,
To watch the veil of night withdrawn,
  And feel the fresh wind blowing.

The murmur of the falls I hear,
  Its night-long vigil keeping ;
And softly now, as if in fear
To rouse their neighbours slumbering near,
  The trees wake from their sleeping.

Dear Lord, such wondrous thoughts of Thee
  My raptured soul are filling,
That, like a bird upon the tree,
With sweet yet wordless minstrelsy
  My inmost heart is thrilling.

# IN THE CHURCHYARD.

As now my feet are straying
   Where all the dead are lying,
O trees, what are ye saying
   That sets my soul a-sighing?

Your sound is as the weeping
   Of one that dreads the morrow,
Or sob of sad heart sleeping
   For fulness of its sorrow.

Methinks your rootlets, groping
   Beneath the dark earth's layers,
Have found the doubt and hoping,
   The blasphemies and prayers,

Of hearts that here are feeding
   The worm ; and now, in pity,
Ye storm with interceding
   The floor of God's great city.

# THE CRIPPLE.

I MET once, in a country lane,
   A little cripple, pale and thin,
Who from my presence sought again
   The shadows she had hidden in.

Her wasted cheeks the sunset skies
   Had hallowed with their fading glow ;
And in her large and lustrous eyes
   There dwelt a child's unuttered woe.

She crept into the autumn wood,
   The parted bushes closed behind ;
Poor little heart, I understood
   The shameless shame that filled her mind.

I understood, and loved her well
   For one sad face I loved of yore, —
And down the lane the dead leaves fell,
   Like dreams that pass for evermore.

# A NOCTURNE.

In the little French church at the bend of the river,
  When rainy and loud was the wind in the night,
An altar-lamp burnt to the mighty Grace-giver,
  The Holy Child Jesus—the Light of the Light.

It was hung on a chain from the roof, and was
    swinging,
  As if the unseemly commotion to chide,
Like the choir-master's baton when hushing the sing-
    ing,
  Or the tongue of the bell when its tollings subside.

It lit up the poor paper flowers on the altar,
  And odd were the shadows it scattered around
On pulpit and lectern, on choir-seat and psalter,
  While the chains threw the ghost of a cross on the
    ground.

The people at home in their cabins were sleeping,
  The curé was tucked in his four-posted bed ;
While under the willows the river was creeping
  As if silent with fear of the wind overhead.

But the little dark church had its own congregation—
  The shadows that swayed on the pews and the
    floor—
While' the rafters that creaked were a choir whose
    laudation
  Had an organ for base in the hurricane's roar.

The rusty gilt cock on the flèche was the preacher,
  And scolding and grumpy his voice was to hear,
As he turned to the storm like some faithful old
    teacher
  Who prophesies hard things regardless of fear.

But the service reflected the state of the weather,
  For though each, I must say, did his part with a
    will,
The preacher and choir spoke and sang all together,
  And the shapes on the benches would never sit
    still.

Yet there was the Host, in the midst of the altar,
   Where that little red curtain of damask was hung,—
The God whom King David has praised in the
      psalter,
   And to whom the whole choir of the ages has sung.

But so big is the heart of our God, the Life-giver,
   That in it life's humour and pathos both meet ;
So I doubt not that night in the church by the river,
   The poor old storm's service to Him sounded
      sweet.

# SONNETS.

## TO MY WIFE.

Sweet Lady, queen-star of my life and thought,
Whose honour, heart and name are one with mine,
Who dost above life's troubled currents shine
With such clear beam as oftentimes hath brought
The storm-tossed spirit into harbours wrought
By love and peace on life's rough margin-line ;
I wish no wish which is not wholly thine,
I hope no hope but what thyself hast sought.
Thou losest not, my Lady, in the wife,
The golden love-light of our earlier days ;
Time dims it not, it mounteth like the sun,
Till earth and sky are radiant.   Sweet, my life
Lies at thy feet, and all life's gifts and praise,
Yet are they nought to what thy knight hath won.

# A CYPRESS WREATH.

### I.

DEATH met a little child beside the sea ;
  The child was ruddy and his face was fair,
  His heart was gladdened with the keen, salt air,
Full of the young waves' laughter and their glee.
Then Death stooped down and kissed him, saying:
    "Thee,
  My child, will I give summers rare and bright,
  And flowers, and morns with never noon or night,
Or clouds to darken, if thou'lt come with me."
Then the child gladly gave his little hand,
And walked with Death along the shining sand,
  And prattled gaily, full of hope, and smiled
As a white mist curled round him on the shore
And hid the land and sea for evermore—
  Death hath no terrors for a little child.

II.

There lived two souls who only lived for love :
  The one a maiden, full of joy and youth,
  The other her young lord, a man of truth
And very valiant.  Them did God above
Knit with those holy bands none may remove
  Save He that formed them.  But next year there
      came
  God's angel, with his face and wings of flame,
And bore the young wife's soul off like a dove.
Then did her lord, disconsolate many years,
  Cry bitterly to God to make them one,
    And take his life, and silence the sweet past.
So Death came tenderly and stilled his tears,
  Clad as a priest, and 'neath the winter's sun
    In a white grave re-wedded them at last.

Quoth Death to Life : " Behold what strength is mine,
    All others perish, yet I do not fail,
    Where life aboundeth most, I most prevail,
I mete out all things with my measuring line."
Then answered Life : "O boastful Death, not thine
    The final triumph, what thy hands undo
    My busy anvil forgeth out anew,
For one lamp darkened, I bring two to shine."
Then answered Death : " Thy handiwork is fair,
    But a slight breath will crumble it to dust."
" Nay, Death," said Life, "for in the vernal air
    A sweeter blossom breaks the winter's crust."
Then God called down and stopped the foolish strife ;
His servants both, for God made Death and Life.

# COLUMBUS.

He caught the words which ocean thunders hurled
  On heedless eastern coasts, in days gone by,
  And to his dreams the ever-westering sky
The ensign of a glorious hope unfurled :
So, onward to the line of mists which curled
  Around the setting sun, with steadfast eye,
  He pushed his course, and, trusting God on high,
Threw wide the portals of a larger world.

The heart that watched through those drear autumn
        nights
    The wide, dark sea, and man's new empire sought,
      Alone, uncheered, hath wrought a deed sublime,
Which, like a star behind the polar lights,
    Will shine through splendours of man's utmost
        thought,
      Down golden eras to the end of time.

1892.

## IDOLS.

In each man's heart a secret temple stands
  For rites idolatrous of praise and prayer :
  And dusky idols through the incensed air,
On single thrones, or grouped in curious bands,
Gaze at the lamp which swings in memory's hands,—
  Some richly carved, with face of beauty rare,
  Some with brute heads and bosoms foul and bare,
Yet crowned with gold and gems from distant lands.

Take now thy torch, descend the winding years,
  The silent stair-way to thy secret shrine,
    And see what Dagon crowns the topmost shelf
With front aggressive, served through hopes and fears
  In ceaseless cult by love that counts divine
    His every blemish,—is not Dagon SELF ?

# SOLOMON.

A DOUBLE line of columns, white as snow,
  And vaulted with mosaics rich in flowers,
  Makes square this cypress grove where fountain
      showers
From golden basins cool the grass below ;
While from that archway strains of music flow,
  And laughings of fair girls beguile the hours.
  But brooding, like one held by evil powers,
The great King heeds not, pacing sad and slow.

His heart hath drained earth's pleasures to the lees,
Hath quivered with life's finest ecstasies :
  Yet now some power reveals as in a glass
The soul's unrest and death's dark mysteries,
  And down the courts the scared slaves watch him
      pass,
  Reiterating, " *Omnia Vanitas !* "

H

## OUT OF THE STORM.

The huge winds gather on the midnight lake,
   Shaggy with rain and loud with foam-white feet,
   Then bound through miles of darkness till they
      meet
The harboured ships and city's squares, and wake
From steeples, domes and houses sounds that take
   A human speech, the storm's mad course to greet;
   And nightmare voices through the rain and sleet
Pass shrieking, till the town's rock-sinews shake.

Howl, winds, around us in this gas-lit room!
   Wild lake, with thunders beat thy prison bars!
   A brother's life is ebbing fast away.
And, mounting on your music through the gloom,
   A pure soul mingles with the morning stars,
     And with them melts into the blaze of day.

St. Luke's Hospital,
    Duluth, May 17th, 1894.

www.ingramcontent.com/pod-product-compliance
Lightning Source LLC
Chambersburg PA
CBHW022340020726
47500CB00004B/1206